Angelina's Baby Sister

Story by **Katharine Holabird** Illustrations by **Helen Craig**

PUFFIN

Angelina was so excited. Very soon there was going to be a new baby in the family! Angelina couldn't wait to be a big sister, and it was hard to think about anything else – even when Miss Lilly gave Angelina a beautiful china statue as a prize at ballet school.

"Perhaps you can make up a dance to welcome the baby," suggested Miss Lilly when Angelina thanked her. Angelina raced home to show her mother the lovely prize.

To my sisters, Jean, Polly and Lisa   KH

For Katharine, with love and thanks for years of fun with Angelina   HC

PUFFIN BOOKS

Published by the Penguin Group: London, New York, Ireland, Australia, Canada, India, New Zealand and South Africa
Penguin Books Ltd, Registered Offices: 80 Strand, London WC2R 0RL, England

www.penguin.com

First published by ABC, All Books for Children, a division of The Children's Company Ltd, 1991
Published by Viking and in Puffin Books 2001
Published in this edition 2006
1 3 5 7 9 10 8 6 4 2
Copyright © HIT Entertainment plc, 2001
Text copyright © Katharine Holabird, 1991
Illustrations copyright © Helen Craig Ltd, 1991
Angelina, Angelina Ballerina and the Dancing Angelina logo are trademarks of HIT Entertainment plc,
Katharine Holabird and Helen Craig Ltd. Angelina is registered in the UK, Japan and US Pat. & Tm. Off.
The Dancing Angelina logo is registered in the UK.
All rights reserved.
Manufactured in China by South China Printing Co. Ltd.
ISBN-13: 978–0–141–38237–1
ISBN-10: 0–141–38237–6

To find out more about Angelina Ballerina, visit her website at **www.angelinaballerina.com**

Angelina ran so fast that she almost bumped into Dr Tuttle as he was leaving. "Your mother is resting upstairs," he said, "and she has a surprise for you …"

Angelina leaped up the stairs and into the bedroom – and there were her parents, gazing lovingly at the newborn baby.

"Her name is Polly," said Mrs Mouseling happily. "Would you like to hold her?" Angelina couldn't believe how delicate her little sister was.

"I'll be a good big sister, Polly," Angelina said softly, as she rocked the baby in her arms.

Angelina's father smiled at her. "We know you will," he said.

That evening Angelina and her father
made supper while Mrs Mouseling
stayed in bed with Polly.

"Don't worry. Pretty soon your
mother will be up and around
again," said Angelina's father,
"but now we have to take
good care of her."

Angelina felt sad and confused. Why should one little baby need so much attention and make her mother feel so tired?

Angelina played with the pretty china dancer. Before she went to sleep she placed it carefully on her chest of drawers where she could show it to her mother.

But the next day Angelina's mother was so busy looking after the new baby that there was no time to look at Angelina's prize, and the day after that Polly sneezed several times and Dr Tuttle came back to see that she didn't catch a cold.

Mr Mouseling was a good cook, but Angelina
missed her mother's special Cheddar cheese
pies after school. Having a baby sister
was not at all the way Angelina
had imagined it would be!

A whole week went by. Angelina
went to school every day and
tried to be good while
everyone fussed over
Polly, but it was
very hard.

The weekend came, and Angelina's grandparents arrived to visit. Angelina could hardly wait to see them again. When the doorbell rang she raced to answer it. "Grandma! Grandpa!" she shouted. "Just look at this!"

Angelina started to show her grandparents her new dance, but Grandma hugged Angelina quickly and said, "Wait just a minute, Angelina dear, first we have to see the baby!"

They went upstairs and Angelina could hear everyone laughing and talking together. She stamped her foot as loudly as she could, but nobody heard her. She tried to do a few steps of her dance but it seemed stupid and clumsy. Upstairs Grandpa was tickling Polly's toes.

"Isn't she just adorable!" Grandma exclaimed.

"Angelina – come and join us!" called her father. But Angelina didn't want to go and see Polly. At that moment she hated Polly and wished Polly would just disappear!

Angelina was so upset that she stomped to her room and slammed the door. Still nobody came. Angelina felt absolutely miserable. She was sure that nobody cared about her any more. Grandma and Grandpa didn't even want to see her dance!

Angelina grabbed one of her
stuffed toys and threw it as hard
as she could across the room,
where it landed with a thud.
Then she threw another and
another. Angelina threw all
of her stuffed toys and all of
her dolls. Then she threw all
her paper and crayons. She
jumped up and down on her
bed and she gave her chest of
drawers a terrific kick. The chest
of drawers shook, and down fell
the china dancer, where it broke
on the floor and lay in pieces.

"ANGELINA!"

Everyone was standing at the door. Angelina threw herself on her bed and burst into tears. Mrs Mouseling sat down on the bed and took Angelina in her arms.

"You were just as sweet as Polly when you were a baby," Angelina's mother smiled, "but now that you're bigger and we can do things together I love you more than ever."

"I just wanted to do my new dance and show you my beautiful prize – but I got so angry I broke it!" Angelina pointed at the broken china dancer and cried even harder.

"I know someone who can fix it," said Mrs Mouseling,
and she gave the little figure to Grandpa,
who went off to get the glue.

"You promised to show us a dance,"
Grandma said, smiling, "and
we've been waiting all
this time."

Slowly Angelina began to feel better. "I guess it's not so
easy to get used to being a big sister," she admitted, wiping
her tears away. Grandma and Grandpa helped Angelina
pick up her toys and they all went downstairs for tea.

Mrs Mouseling had baked Angelina's favourite Cheddar cheese pies. "I wanted to surprise you," she said.

Then Mr Mouseling played his fiddle and Angelina did her special dance to welcome her baby sister, while Polly giggled with delight.

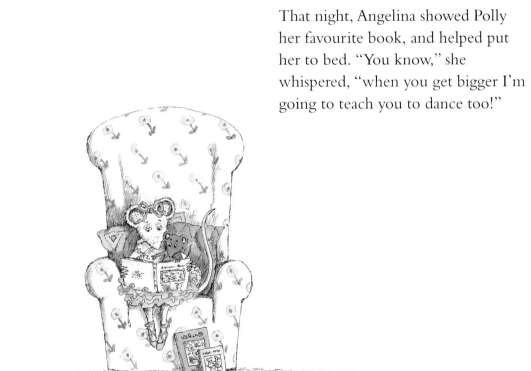

That night, Angelina showed Polly her favourite book, and helped put her to bed. "You know," she whispered, "when you get bigger I'm going to teach you to dance too!"